THE BULLY FROM THE
BLACK LAGOON

STORY BY
MIKE THALER

PICTURES BY
JARED LEE

Cartwheel
B·O·O·K·S ®

SCHOLASTIC INC.

New York   Toronto   London   Auckland   Sydney
Mexico City   New Delhi   Hong Kong   Buenos Aires

visit us at www.abdopublishing.com

Reinforced library bound edition published in 2012 by Spotlight,
a division of the ABDO Group, PO Box 398166, Minneapolis, MN 55439. Spotlight produces high-quality
reinforced library bound editions for schools and libraries. Published by agreement with Scholastic Inc.

Printed in the United States of America, North Mankato, Minnesota.
102011
012012
This book contains at least 10% recycled materials.

To Ron and Joan
Always faithful love
— M.T.

To Spencer Andrew Lee
— J.L.

Text copyright © 2004 by Mike Thaler. Illustrations copyright © 2004 by Jared D. Lee Studio, Inc.
All rights reserved. Published by Scholastic Inc. SCHOLASTIC, CARTWHEEL BOOKS, and
associated logos are trademarks and/or registered trademarks of Scholastic Inc.

Library of Congress Cataloging-in-Publication Data

This book was previously cataloged with the following information:

Thaler, Mike, 1936-
  The bully from the Black Lagoon / by Mike Thaler ; pictures by Jared Lee.
     p.   cm.
[1. Fear —Juvenile fiction. 2. Schools —Juvenile fiction. 3. Bullying in schools —Juvenile fiction.]
PZ7.T3 Bul 2004
[E}-dc22

                              2005274632

ISBN 978-1-59961-953-8 (reinforced library edition)

All Spotlight books are reinforced library bindings
and manufactured in the United States of America.

There's a new kid in our school. His name is Butch Pounder, and he's supposed to be a terrible bully.

I haven't seen him yet, but I heard he's almost as big as Coach Kong. At his old school, he was on the football team.

In fact, he *was* the football team.

He was sent to the principal's office so often that he had his own desk there.

They say he transferred from the state pen and has a record.

Rumor has it that he beat up every single kid
in his old school twice and ate the teacher's pet.

I don't want to get beaten up even once!

I can see it now—in art class he'll take all the crayons.

In the library he'll take all the books.

 In the cafeteria he'll take our lunch money and eat all the food.

At recess he'll put little kids into orbit
by sitting on the seesaw.

Then he'll kick *us* in kickball, sock *us* in soccer,
and use *us* for bases in baseball.
After recess we'll have to be *recess-itated*.

At our school dance he'll be the punch.

And at our school carnival he'll be the carnivore!

We'll spend half our time in the nurse's office
and the other half hiding in our lockers.

BROKEN ARM

BROKEN LEG

BROKEN HEART

On the school bus he'll take up all the seats.
We'll just stand with our crutches in the aisles.

Then he'll get off at my stop, follow me home,
and eat my snack. What will I do?

I can lift weights and learn *carrot-tea* and *kung phooey*—which will make my hands into lethal weapons. "AA-YAAH!"

I can take Tailspin to school. He could lick 'im!

Or I could just wear armor!

With my luck, he'll sit right behind me in class.
Then he'll push, pull, poke, and pinch me all day.
And if I tell Mrs. Green, he'll ram, slam, jam,
and bam me after school.

I know what I'll do...I'll practice running.
I'll become so fast that he'll never catch me.
I'll start right now.

I run down the hall, turn the corner—and *WHAM*!

I bump right into BUTCH POUNDER! Oh no, he *is* big!
I bounce right off of him.

He picks me up with one hand....

"My name is Butch," he smiles. "I just transferred from the state of Pennsylvania, and I'm new in school."
"My name's Hubie," I grin. "I'm old in school."

"I'm lost," he sighs. "Do you know where Mrs. Green's class is?"

"I sure do," I answer. "Follow me. By the way, Butch, do you really have a record?"

"Yeah, I have lots of records," he smiles. "And a record player."

"Cool. Could I hear them sometime?" I ask.

RECORD

"Sure, Hubie, if you promise not to run into me anymore," he laughs.

"Deal!" I smile as we walk down the hall, shaking hands.